D0041825

Look for these

ROTTEN SCHOOL
books, too!

ROTTEN SCHOOL

GROWTH · LEARNING · PIZZA!

DUMB CLUCKS

R.L. STINE

Illustrations by Trip Park

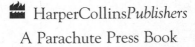

HarperCollins*Publishers*

A Parachute Press Book

For Cameron
–TP

Dumb Clucks

Copyright © 2007 by Parachute Publishing, L.L.C.

Cover copyright © 2007 by Parachute Publishing, L.L.C.

All rights reserved.

No part of this book may be used or reproduced in any manner whatsoever without written permission except in the case of brief quotations embodied in critical articles and reviews. Printed in the United States of America.

For information address HarperCollins Children's Books, a division of HarperCollins Publishers, 1350 Avenue of the Americas, New York, NY 10019.

www.harpercollinschildrens.com

Library of Congress Cataloging-in-Publication Data is available.

ISBN 978-0-06-123278-7 (trade bdg.) —ISBN 978-0-06-123279-4 (lib. bdg.)

Cover and interior design by mjcdesign

1 2 3 4 5 6 7 8 9 10

❖

First Edition

—: CONTENTS :—

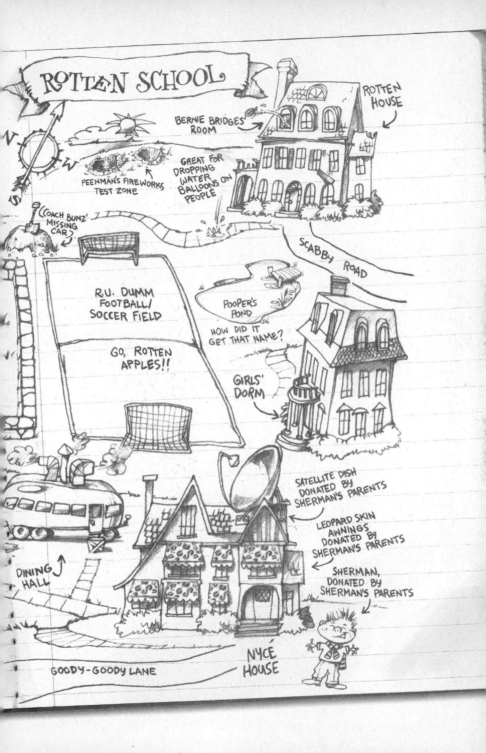

MORNING ANNOUNCEMENTS

Good morning, Rotten Students. This is Headmaster Upchuck, wishing you a Rotten day in every way. I have today's morning announcements.

But first I have a reminder for those students who are trying to drown out my voice by barking like a dog. Many students are interested in what I have to say, so please be courteous.

BARK BARK BARKBARK!
BARK BARK BARK!

Who was that? Get his name. I want that stopped. I mean it. It's not funny.

Here are today's important announcements. Please listen carefully.

BARK BARK BARKBARK!
BARK BARK BARK!

The meeting of the After-School "No Members Allowed" Club was canceled because no one showed up.

This message from Chef Baloney. He wants all students who complained about last night's dinner to know that monkey brains are considered a *treat* in some parts of the world.

Our science teacher, Mr. M.T. Beeker, has an urgent message: Eight monkeys are missing from the science lab. If anyone knows where they are, please contact Mr. Beeker.

Coach Manley Bunz has figured out why our first-grade softball team is such a big loser. He would like to remind team members that your head is used in *soccer*—not softball.

Fifth-grade class clown Harry Sholders will be demonstrating how to send your sneeze flying across the table at lunch today.

Our librarian, Ms. Shuttup, reminds all students that the Rotten School books by R.L. Stine are not allowed in this school because they are filled with lies, lies, *LIES!*

Chapter 1

ME'RE NOT MMMMINTO MMMMADPOLES

Seven o'clock at night is homework hour in Rotten House, our dorm. So I knew where to find all my friends: downstairs in the Commons Room—our living room—watching TV.

We don't do our homework at night. We do it in the five minutes before class starts in the morning. That way, it's still fresh in our minds.

That leaves more time for important things like watching TV, playing video games, and snapping your fingers in your friends' faces to make them flinch.

You probably do your homework at home. But we don't go home, because Rotten School is a boarding school. That means we live here.

I'm Bernie Bridges. I bet you know me because I'm in the Fourth Grader Hall of Fame.

I know. I know. There *is* no Fourth Grader Hall of Fame.

But if there was, I'd be in it.

I don't like to brag, but I'm the dude who knows how to get the *most* out of fourth grade.

The most *money*, that is.

Tonight I was planning a special sale of awesome T-shirts. I piled the shirts up on a cart and wheeled them into the Commons Room.

I knew my buddies would be fighting over them, *begging* me to let them each buy four or five shirts.

"All right. Line up, dudes!" I shouted. I wheeled my cart in front of the TV.

All my Rotten House pals were there. Feenman, Crench, Belzer, Chipmunk, Beast, Nosebleed...

I rubbed my hands together. I was already counting my money.

"Listen up, guys," I said. "Did you know it's a

holiday? It's Lucky T-Shirt Day. And every shirt I have on this cart is a lucky shirt!"

"Bernie, you're blocking the TV," Crench said.

"You can't watch TV while I'm having this special sale," I said. "Half off every T-shirt! Get up, dudes. Check 'em out!"

"Bernie, you're blocking the TV," Feenman said.

"Guys, you don't understand," I said. "I've got your favorites here. Look! *Tweenage Mutant Ninja Tadpoles* shirts. Only five dollars!"

I grabbed Crench by the shoulders and tried to hoist him out of his chair. But he plopped right back down. "Bernie, I can't see the TV."

"Up. Up! Everyone up!" I shouted, clapping my hands. "I've got the Tadpoles, dudes! I know you're totally into *Tweenage Mutant Ninja Tadpoles*."

They stared at the screen.

My friend Beast opened his mouth wide and let out a deafening burp. It lasted about two minutes. Big chunks of food flew from his mouth and sprayed the room.

Normally, a burp that good would make my pals laugh for *hours*.

Tonight they stared at the TV screen. No one even blinked.

"Okay, okay," I said. "You drive a hard bargain. You can have the shirts for *four-fifty* each!"

I held up a T-shirt. "Look, dudes. You can wear your favorite Tadpole. Hey—who wants Herman? I've got Herman shirts. Who wants Murray? Sidney? Melvin? Melvin is your *hero*—right, Feenman?"

Feenman stared at the TV.

"Here's a winner," I said, pulling a shirt from the bottom of the pile. "This shirt has all *twenty-four* Tadpoles on it! Even Myron, the Shy Tadpole. Check it out!"

Silence.

Then … more silence.

Finally my friend Nosebleed spoke up. "Mernie, me're not mmmminto mmmmadpoles," he said.

"Huh? Nosebleed, what *language* are you speaking?" I asked.

"MmmmI'm mmmeaking English," he said. "I mmmave ummmph tissues stuffed in mmmmy nose. I mmmmhave a nosebleed."

Poor guy. Everything gives him a nosebleed. Tying

his *shoes* gives him a nosebleed! When the sun sets, it gives him a nosebleed!

"Bernie, Nosebleed was trying to tell you something," Feenman said. "We're not into the Tadpoles anymore. Too babyish! We're into a *new* show."

"Hel-lo?" I cried. "A *new* show? You, TRAITORS! I've got *three dozen* shirts with these slimy Tadpoles on them!"

Feenman shrugged. "Babyish."

"Okay, tell me," I said through gritted teeth. "What show are you traitors watching now?"

"We'll give you a hint," Crench said.

And they all chimed in at once, singing...
BLUCK BLUCK BLUCK BLUCK BLUCK BLUCK BLUCK BLUCK BLUCK BLUCK BLUCK BLUCK.

Chapter 2

A Birdbrain That Thinks

BLUCK. BLUCK. BLUCK. BLUCK.
BLUCK. BLUCK. BLUCK. BLUCK. BLUCK
BLUCK. BLUCK. BLUCK.

I waited for them to stop BLUCKing. It took a long time.

Nosebleed blucked so hard, he got another nose-bleed.

Finally they fell back on their chairs, gasping for breath.

"The name of the new show is *Bluck?*" I asked.

Everyone groaned.

"No way," Feenman said. "Bernie, everyone is watching *Stupid Chicken*."

"He's totally awesome," Crench said. "He has Drumsticks of Doom!"

"And Buffalo Wings of Steel," Belzer added.

I turned to Chipmunk. He's the shyest kid in school. He had a blindfold pulled down over his eyes. Chipmunk only *listens* to TV. He's too shy to watch it.

"Chipmunk, *you're* loyal to the Tadpoles—aren't you?" I asked.

Chipmunk cleared his throat for about ten minutes. It's one of his most disturbing habits. "The Tadpoles are kinda violent," he whispered. He started to tremble.

"Bernie, don't you watch *Stupid Chicken*?" Belzer asked. "It's the most popular cartoon on Chickelodeon."

"It comes on every night after *Teriyaki Chicken*," Feenman said. "You know. The Karate Klucker?"

"Huh?" I stared at the TV screen. There was Stupid Chicken. A fat, yellow chicken in a blue and red cape. He flew across the sky, blucking his head off.

"I don't believe you dudes are sitting here watching

a flying chicken," I said. "How *could* you abandon the Tadpoles?"

The chicken flew into some kind of house made of ice. "Who lives there?" I asked. "Frozen Chicken?"

The guys usually love my jokes. But nobody even smiled.

"That's the Henhouse of Solitude," Crench said. "That's where Stupid Chicken goes to think things over."

I rolled my eyes. "Oh, perfect. A birdbrain that *thinks*!"

I stared at the screen. "What's that dumb-looking featherball rolling behind Stupid Chicken?" I asked. "Something he coughed up after breakfast?"

Beast jumped to his feet and shook a fist at me.

His fist was bigger than my head! "Are you making fun of America's National Chicken?" he boomed.

"Of course not," I said. I took several steps back. Beast can

be dangerous. Especially if he hasn't had his rabies shots.

"That featherball is Little Cluck-Cluck," Feenman said. "He's always getting into trouble. He's so funny."

I stared at my worthless pile of T-shirts. "Ha-ha," I said bitterly.

What was I gonna do with these shirts?

Maybe I could take a marker and draw feathers on the Tadpoles. I'd tell the guys it's what Stupid Chicken looked like when he was a baby.

No. No way they'd believe it.

"Crench, tell me," I said. "How can a chicken be a superhero?"

"Are you kidding?" Crench said. "First he pecks your knees to bring you down. Then he kicks gravel on you."

"Exciting," I muttered.

I slapped the pile of T-shirts. I *had* to sell them to *somebody*!

Suddenly I had an idea.

The first graders LOVE the Tadpoles. And they're gonna LOVE these shirts!

I pushed my cart out of the dorm and raised my binoculars to my eyes. "First graders! Where are you? Where *are* you?"

Chapter 3

CLUCK-BLUCK-LUCK?

I spotted a whole bunch of the little dudes on R.U. Dumm Field. That's our soccer field.

It must have been their evening gym class. But I couldn't tell what kind of game they were playing. They were running around in crazy circles, flapping their arms.

Coach Manley Bunz was blowing his whistle so hard, he was as red as a tomato. His eyes bulged at least an *inch* out of his head.

I wheeled my T-shirt cart onto the grass. "Coach Bunz—what's wrong?" I shouted.

"GULLLLP!" Coach made a strange sound. Then he started dancing around with his tongue flapping, going, "Unnh unnnh unnh."

"Coach? Coach, did I startle you?" I asked.

I finally guessed the problem. He had swallowed his whistle.

I slapped him on the back till the whistle came flying out, along with his breakfast. He wiped the whistle off with a handkerchief and started blowing it again.

The first graders were still running around in crazy circles, flapping their arms, and ...CLUCKING?

"Coach Bunz, what's up with this?" I asked. "What game are they playing?"

"It . . . it's supposed to be soccer," he bellowed. "But they're all pretending to be *chickens*!"

"No way," I muttered. I ran over to two little dudes who were having an argument.

"He says it like this," the first kid said. "Cluck-luck-luck. Cluck-luck-luck."

"You're joking!" the other kid shouted. "He goes Cluck-*bluck*-luck. Cluck-*bluck*-luck."

"You're a jerk! He does not!"

A third kid—a big, beefy, redheaded bruiser—pushed the other two kids aside. "You're both stupid," he growled. "Little Cluck-Cluck goes Cluck-bluck-gluck-luck-pluck-luck-gluck. *Everyone* knows that! It's Cluck-bluck-gluck-luck-pluck-luck-gluck."

They all began blucking and glucking their heads off. But I wasn't listening.

I stared goggle-eyed at their T-shirts.

Yes. You guessed it. They were *all* wearing white shirts with a fat, yellow blob on the front.

And that fat, yellow blob was . . . Little Cluck-Cluck!

"Dudes! Dudes!" I shouted. I waved my hands over my head to get them quiet. "Dudes—you all know me, right? You all know I'm in the Fourth Grader Hall of Fame—right?"

"Cluck cluck," the big redheaded dude sneered.

"Listen to me, guys!" I shouted. "You all know me. I'm the guy who sells you tickets to the sunset every night. I wouldn't lie to you—would I?"

"Cluck cluck," the kid repeated. What a joker.

"*The Tweenage Mutant Ninja Tadpoles* are much more awesome than Stupid Chicken!" I shouted. "Little Cluck-Cluck is a dumb cluck! The Tadpoles rule!"

"Peck him!" the redheaded kid growled. "He can't say that about the Courageous Caped Cluck-Cluck!"

"Peck him! Peck him!"

Other kids took up the shout.

They all rushed forward, clucking and blucking and glucking. "Peck him! Peck him!"

I couldn't back away. I was trapped inside a circle of clucking, flapping first graders.

"Dudes, check out these shirts! Here's Herbie, the Sneezy Tadpole! You love him—right? How about Norman, the Hungry Tadpole. Isn't it funny how he's always hungry? Who wants to buy—"

They pushed the cart over. Then they dove at me.

"OW! OW! OW!"

That was me, yelling in pain.

They pecked my arms and legs. They pecked my chest and my back. They pecked the top of my head!

I went down on the ground. They turned their backs and started to do a chicken strut, kicking dirt and grass on me.

"Help! Coach Bunz! Help me!" I cried.

He was blowing his whistle too loud to hear me.

Was this the end of Bernie B.?

Chapter 4

THE UPCHUCK CALLS

I rolled myself into a tight ball and hugged my knees.

Finally the clucking and pecking stopped. Someone tapped my shoulder.

I slowly let go of my knees and looked up. "Belzer!"

"Hi, Bernie," he said. He flashed me his crooked smile. "How's it going?"

"Not great," I said. I sat up with a groan.

Belzer brushed the dirt and grass off my shoulders. "That's nice of you to play with first graders," he said.

"I love spending time with the little guys," I said.

I checked out my bruises and bites. "How'd you get rid of them?"

"I told them they could have the Tadpole shirts for free," he said.

I swallowed hard.

"They grabbed them and ran away as fast as they could," Belzer said.

"Cute kids," I said. I gazed around. "And where's my cart?"

"They took that, too," Belzer replied. "Some of them pushed it, and some of them rode in it."

"Sounds like fun," I said. I stood up and let Belzer brush the dirt and grass off my pants.

"I have a message for you, Big B," Belzer said. "From Headmaster Upchuck. He wants to see you— right away."

My heart turned to ice. I had to pound my chest with both fists to thaw it out and get it pumping again.

"He probably wants to give me some kind of award," I told Belzer. "Maybe he wants to name me *Student of the Decade* or something. I'll bet there's a big CASH PRIZE, too."

"Maybe he wants to toss you out on your butt," Belzer said.

"Maybe," I agreed.

Headmaster Upchuck lives in a little white house next to the classroom building. His office is on the first floor.

A sign next to the entrance reads:

But the house is surrounded by an electric barbed-wire fence. The front yard is filled with big poison ivy shrubs. Two snarling guard dogs patrol the fence. And the welcome mat at the front door says:

I could be wrong. But I get the feeling the Headmaster doesn't really want to see us.

Maybe he's shy because of his height. He's only about three feet tall. He could be mistaken for one of the students. Except that he's as bald as a cantaloupe and wears a gray wool suit every day.

And now he wanted to see me. Why was I in trouble? My brain did flips, then flops.

He couldn't know about my secret for getting free Nutty Nutty candy bars by removing the *back* of the candy machine.

He couldn't know about how I wrote the answers to the math test on the lenses of my sunglasses.

He couldn't know about my all-night, wet towel–snapping contests. And he couldn't know that I was the one who *accidentally* dropped water balloons on five teachers.

So, why was I in trouble with The Upchuck?

I dug my way under the electric fence. Then I jumped over the poison ivy shrubs. I fed two pounds of raw hamburger to the guard dogs to keep them busy.

And I stepped up to the front door and rang the bell.

Chapter 5

No Stink Bomb, No Naughty Words

A few seconds later, I heard someone on the other side of the door undoing the thirty-four locks. Headmaster Upchuck himself pulled open the door.

"Bernie, my lad. Come in. Come in," he said cheerfully.

Uh-oh. That meant I was in *major* trouble.

"Sir, I had *nothing* to do with the stink bomb during the *Good Citizenship* assembly," I said. "That was a terrible shame. All those kids throwing up on our guest speaker like that. I hope you catch the person who did that."

"Bernie, come into my office," The Upchuck said, still grinning. "You know my door is always open to all students."

He carefully locked all thirty-four locks.

I followed him into his office. He had a tiny desk and tiny desk chair. It looked like doll furniture.

"Sir, can I help you tie your necktie?" I asked. "I know you're not quite tall enough to reach your neck."

"No, thank you," he said.

"Sir, that wasn't *me* who sang the naughty words to our school song," I said. "I don't approve of that at all."

"Sit down, Bernie," the Headmaster said. He pointed to a little chair in front of his little desk.

I lowered myself into it. My knees hit my lips!

"Sir, I didn't make those dog barking sounds during the Morning Announcements yesterday," I said. "I know it *sounded* like me. But it wasn't."

Upchuck rubbed his bald head till it was as shiny as a bowling ball. "Bernie, you're not in trouble," he said.

"Of course not, sir," I said. "I try to be a perfect student."

"In fact, I have a *very big* job for you," he said.

Uh-oh.

Now I KNEW I was in major trouble!

Upchuck Does a Happy Dance

"A job, sir?" I said. "Well, if you'd like me to take over the Headmaster job for a day or two, I'm sure I could do it. But we'd *miss* you, sir. We'd miss you a lot!"

He rubbed his head till it glowed like a lightbulb. "No, Bernie. That's not the job," he said. "I'm naming you head of the Parents' Day Committee."

I swallowed my gum.

"Wh-who else is on the committee?" I stammered.

"Nobody," Upchuck said. "I'm putting you in charge because you're the biggest troublemaker on campus."

I could feel myself blushing. "You're too kind, sir."

A grin spread over The Upchuck's shiny face. "See, Bernie? This is your last chance. If you *fail* at this job, I will pack your bags for you."

"Pack my bags, sir?"

"Yes. And I'll do cartwheels across the Great Lawn," he said. "Because I'll be sending you home for good. "YAAAAAAY!"

He hopped onto his desk and did a wild dance.

"Hel-lo! Fail at this job?" I cried. "I don't think so. I don't know the *meaning* of the word *fail*."

He stopped dancing. "Don't spoil my fun," he muttered.

"Sir, what exactly is my job?" I asked.

He dropped back into his doll chair. "Your job is to make sure everything stays calm and quiet at this school for Parents' Day. If anything goes wrong— *anything* at all…"

"Sir, how could anything go wrong?" I said. "My middle name is Calm and Quiet. I'll make you proud, sir. Proud you named me chairman."

"Bernie, shut up," Upchuck said.

"Okay, sir. You got it!" I flashed him a two-finger salute.

The Headmaster handed me a big shopping bag. "Bernie, these are the Parents' Day invitations for the parents," he said. "Angel Goodeboy works in my office three days a week. He already addressed all these invitations."

"Goodeboy is a good boy!" I said.

"I want you to mail them to the parents," Upchuck continued.

"No prob, sir," I said. "I'll get Belzer right on that."

"There's more to this job," The Upchuck said. "I think you'll like this part, Bernie. I need you to raise a lot of money. We need the best snacks and refreshments money can buy."

"For *me*, sir?" I said. "Oh no. You don't have to pay me with snacks. I'm happy to do my duty and serve my school and—"

"Shut up, Bernie," Upchuck said.

I gave him another salute.

"You need to raise money to put out fabulous food

for the parents. I really want to impress them."

I nodded. "And we should dress all the kids right to make it a very special day. Every single student should wear a *Tweenage Mutant Ninja Tadpoles* shirt— right, sir? I just happen to have a few..."

Upchuck jumped to his feet. "Time for you to beat it," he said.

He walked me to the door. I could hear the guard dogs growling outside. I wished I'd brought more hamburger meat.

"Bernie, remember," Upchuck said, unlocking the thirty-four locks, "I'll be watching. I want you to get the school calm and quiet *right now*. And keep it calm and quiet from now till Parents' Day."

"Calm and quiet. No prob," I said, saluting him again.

Upchuck shoved me out the door and slammed it behind me.

As I fought off the dogs, my brain was flipping and flopping.

Headmaster Upchuck wanted me to *fail*. He couldn't *wait* to pack my bags and send me home.

But he also gave me an *excuse* to raise as much

money as I could.

Dollar signs floated in front of my eyes. MANY, MANY dollar signs.

Hey! There's *gotta* be a way to cash in on the Stupid Chicken craze *and* make lots of money, I told myself. There's *gotta* be a way ...

Suddenly I had an idea.

Chapter 7

HATCH
YOUR OWN

The next night all my friends sat in front of the TV again. And the cries of "BLUCK~GLUCK~LUCK~BLUCK" rang through Rotten House.

"Yo! Whussup!" I shouted. "I've got what you guys have been waiting for!"

Headmaster Upchuck wanted me to raise refreshment money. Well, he picked the right dude for the job. I carried my big wooden crate into the room and set it down carefully in front of the TV.

On the screen, Stupid Chicken was pecking the life out of an evil worm. The worm wore a black cape. That's how I knew it was evil.

"Bernie, you're blocking the TV," Crench groaned.

"This is better than TV," I said. I pulled up the lid of the crate. "You dudes don't want to sit and *watch* Stupid Chicken all day. You want to *live* the adventure, don't you?"

"Wow! Awesome!" Feenman cried, pointing at the screen. "Stupid Chicken just pecked Wonder Wormboy in two. And now *both worm halves* are fighting Stupid Chicken!"

"Wonder Wormboy?" I said.

"He's not really a worm," Belzer said. "He's a mutant who has the power to *turn* himself into a worm."

"Good choice," I said.

"Know my favorite sandwich?" Beast said. "Worm butter and jelly."

Crench stared at him. "Where do you buy worm butter?" he asked.

Beast chuckled. "You don't buy it— you MAKE it!" he said. "The hard part is pulling it off the bottom of your shoe."

"Dudes! Dudes!" I shouted. "Give me a break here!"

I reached into the crate and pulled out an egg. I had 144 eggs, and I hoped I could sell them all.

"Get your money ready," I said. I held the egg up so they could look at it. "These are special. It's *Hatch Your Own Stupid Chicken!*"

That got their attention. They stared at the egg as if they were hypnotized.

"See this egg?" I said. "There's a Stupid Chicken inside each one."

Nosebleed leaned forward on the couch and squinted at it. "There's a Stupid Chicken in there? No joke?"

"Five dollars," I said. "Five dollars and you can hatch your own."

"Bernie, give us a break," Feenman said. "It's just an egg. You can't charge five dollars for an egg."

I gasped. "Feenman, you wouldn't pay five dollars for Stupid Chicken?" I asked. "I thought you were a big fan."

"Can I ask you a question?" Billy the Brain asked.

We call him Brain because he's the smartest kid in our school. He has a solid C average. And his homework is never more than two weeks late.

He's a genius!

"What's your question, Brain?" I asked.

"Do you have any Little Cluck-Clucks in there?"

"No prob," I said. I held up another egg. "Here's one. Hatch Your Own Little Cluck-Cluck. How many do you want, Brain?"

"Lemme SEE that!" Beast roared. He jumped up from his spot on the floor and tromped over to me.

"Gimme that!" He grabbed the egg from my hand. "Is there really a Stupid Chicken inside this thing?"

He shook it hard, like a salt shaker. Then he crushed the shell in his fist.

I watched the thick, yellow yolk run down his hand.

"HAW HAW HAW!" Beast tossed back his head and HAWed. "I killed Stupid Chicken! HAW HAW HAW!"

He HAWed for another minute or two. We're all afraid to stop him when he starts HAWing.

When Beast finally stopped, Nosebleed shook his head. "It's not funny to joke about Stupid Chicken," he said. "Look. You gave me a nosebleed."

Beast jammed the crushed egg—shell and all—

into his mouth. "Check it out. I'm *eating* Stupid Chicken! HAW HAW HAW!"

Yolk ran down his chin. He made slurping and crunching noises until he swallowed it.

"Not funny!" Nosebleed cried. He grabbed an egg from the crate and shouted, "STUPID CHICKEN TAKES NO PRISONERS!"

And he smashed the egg on top of Beast's head.

CRAAAAAACK! SMUSSSSSSH!

Beast looked stunned for a moment. He wiped egg yolk from his forehead. Then he reached into the crate and grabbed three eggs at once.

With an animal growl, he heaved them at Nosebleed.

And missed.

CRAAAAAACK! SMUSSSSSSH!
CRAAAAAACK! SMUSSSSSSH!
CRAAAAAACK! SMUSSSSSSH!

He hit Chipmunk, Feenman, and Crench instead.

"No WAY!" Feenman cried, pulling egg yolk from his hair.

All three of them dove for my egg crate.

They came up blucking and throwing.
BLUCK~LUCK~GLUCK!
CRAAAAAACK! SMUSSSSSSH!
CRAAAAAACK! SMUSSSSSSH!

This had to stop! I tried to pull the eggs away.

But Beast jammed his big shoe into the crate to hold it down.

Then he heaved eggs across the room as fast as he could throw them.

CRAAAAAACK! SMUSSSSSSH!
CRAAAAAACK! SMUSSSSSSH!

Eggs dripped down the walls. Yellow yolk oozed down the TV screen. Broken shells crackled under our shoes. Our clothes were soaked and sticky.

The battle didn't end until all my eggs were gone.

And that's when Mrs. Heinie walked into the room.

Mrs. Heinie is our dorm mother. One of her main jobs is to keep us from egging each other.

"Oh no! Oh no!" she cried, gazing around the sticky, drippy room through her thick eyeglasses. "Oh no! Oh no!" She pressed her hands against her cheeks. "Oh no! Oh no!"

I knew she would blame me.

As a member of the Fourth Grader Hall of Fame, I always get blamed when something interesting happens.

"Oh no! Oh no!" she cried.

"I can explain, Mrs. Heinie," I said.

She crossed her arms in front of her and squinted at me. "Explain?"

"Yes," I said. "You see, we wanted to cook you a surprise breakfast. Scrambled eggs."

"And ... what happened?" Mrs. Heinie asked.

"We forgot we didn't have a pan!"

Chapter 8

LIKE PICKING YOUR NOSE

Did Mrs. H. believe my story?

Hel-lo. If she had, would I be scrubbing the walls and mopping the floors like this?

Is this a job for a Hall of Famer? I don't think so.

Things were not going well. I was losing money fast. I had spent fifteen dollars for the smashed eggs.

Wasted. All wasted.

I had to beg Mrs. Heinie not to tell Headmaster Upchuck about the egg fight. I was supposed to keep things calm and quiet. So far, I was a failure at that, too.

I needed to start raising money right away. I needed the money for the Parents' Day refreshments. *And* for a private charity I call the Bernie Bridges Private Charity Fund.

I needed some new ideas. I needed to talk to someone brainy.

And who could be brainier than Billy the Brain?

Billy is so smart, he does crossword puzzles without even looking at the clues! He's so smart, he can tell whether it's day or night just by checking the position of the sun.

I knocked on his door and stepped inside. I saw Billy standing on his head in the middle of the room. "Whoa. Why are you doing that?" I asked.

"Doing what?" he asked.

"Standing on your head," I said.

"It's an ancient thing," Billy replied. "People used to do it before they figured out they were upside-down."

"That's interesting," I said. "But why are you doing it now?"

"I don't remember," he said. "Help me to my feet, okay?"

I helped Billy to his feet. "Can I pick your brain?" I asked.

He stared at me. "You mean like picking your nose?"

"No. I didn't mean that. I need some ideas," I said.

Billy slapped me a high five. "You came to the right guy," he said. "I have an average of 235 ideas a day. Not counting weekends."

"Awesome," I said. I dropped down on the edge of his bed. "I need to raise a lot of money. Do you have any good ideas?"

He started to think. He shut his eyes and rubbed his chin. Then he *opened* his eyes and rubbed his chin. Then he tugged his hair and rolled his eyes while rubbing his chin.

"I've *got* it!" he cried. "Why don't you bring Stupid Chicken to Rotten School? Kids would pay a LOT to see Stupid Chicken in person. Bernie, you could probably get ten dollars a ticket!"

My mouth dropped open. "Excuse me?"

Billy slapped me on the back. "You could do it, Bernie. Make a few phone calls. Find Stupid

Chicken's agent. I'll bet you could make a deal to bring Stupid Chicken here."

"I ... I ... I ..." I was speechless. I stood there with my mouth open, going, "I ... I ... I ..."

Finally I put a hand on Billy's shoulder. "Billy," I said softly, "I have very bad news for you."

Billy turned to me. "Bad news?"

I nodded. "Yes. Listen to me. Stupid Chicken isn't real. Stupid Chicken is a *cartoon*."

Billy blinked several times. "Are you *sure?*" he asked.

I took his arm and led him to a chair. Then I quickly left the room. He was panting hard, and his face was as white as a sheep. I could see he was badly shaken. I knew he had to be alone.

I closed the door and stepped out into the hall.

Maybe Billy needs a new nickname, I thought.

How about Billy the Stupid Idiot?

But I couldn't worry about Billy. I had to start raising the big bucks. And I didn't have much time.

Downstairs, I could hear the guys BLUCK BLUCKing away.

Back in my room, I picked up the phone and

made the call that would start me on my way to being RICH.

"Send me three dozen Stupid Chicken shirts," I said. "And three dozen Stupid Chicken caps."

Bernie B. knows a craze when he sees one. I *knew* I could cash in on this chicken craze. How could I lose?

Chapter 9

CHICKEN ON ICE

A few nights later, I called a dorm meeting in my room. The guys came trooping in, punching each other, making each other flinch.

"Can I sit on a chair?" Nosebleed asked. "Sitting on the floor gives me a nosebleed."

"Just sit close," I said, "because you'll want to see what I've got."

I had the Stupid Chicken shirts and caps piled up on my bed. The shirts were a beautiful egg-yolk yellow. They had Stupid Chicken's face on them, with his Buffalo Wings of Steel. And the words: I'M

WITH STUPID CHICKEN in bright red.

The caps were egg shell color. With the words: YOU'VE GOT PLUCK, LITTLE CLUCK-CLUCK on the front in yellow.

Could they be any more awesome?

"Line up, dudes," I said. "Special tonight. Only five dollars for a shirt. And four dollars for a cap. The caps are made of *real* sturdy cardboard. None of that fake stuff. Sorry, but I can only sell *five* per customer!"

They didn't move. I gazed around the room at their blank faces.

"Do you all speak English?" I said. "Didn't you hear me? I've got your favorite here. Check these out. Shirts and caps. Get your money out and line up, guys. Don't push. There's enough for everyone."

Nothing.

They stared at me.

Nosebleed wiped his nose. Beast was eating the foam rubber out of my bed pillow. Feenman and Crench were snapping fingers in each other's faces, making each other flinch.

"Okay, okay," I said. "You drive a hard bargain.

Okay. I'll give you a deal. You can buy a shirt and a cap together for only twelve dollars. How about it?"

I knew they couldn't add five and four. In arithmetic class, most of them hadn't started addition yet. Billy the Brain was trying to figure it out on his fingers.

"Come on. Who's first to look terrific?" I asked, holding up a shirt.

No takers.

"What's going on, guys?" I asked.

Feenman finally spoke up. "Bernie, we have to *save* our money. To buy tickets to *Stupid Chicken On Ice.*"

My mouth dropped open. "Huh? Ice?"

Feenman nodded. "Yeah. It's coming to town next week. We've got to buy our tickets early."

"But, guys," I said, "I'm raising money for Parents' Day. What about your parents?"

"Let them buy their *own* tickets!" Feenman said.

Chapter 10

RAH RAH ROTTEN SCHOOL

Was I discouraged? Does a snake eat his dinner whole?

Trick question! Bernie B. is *never* discouraged.

There are lots of kids on this campus. I just had to find the ones who wanted to wear the snazziest Stupid Chicken shirts and caps on earth.

"Belzer, pick up the shirts and caps," I said. "Follow me."

He piled the shirts so high in front of him, he couldn't see. "Bernie, could you take some of these?" he asked.

"Bad for my back," I said. "Don't worry about it.

You don't have to see. Just follow the sound of my voice."

I sang the *Official Rotten School Song* all the way to the Student Center.

"Rah rah Rotten School!
I'd rather be in Rotten School
than NOT in school…"

It's a totally awesome song. And I knew a lot of my friends listened to it day and night on their computers at www.rottenschool.com.

"Careful, Belzer," I said. "I'll have to make you pay for any shirts you drop."

"But, Bernie," he whined, "you already took all my money in that all-night Ping-Pong game. Remember?"

"Oh. Right," I muttered. "You were a terrible Ping-Pong player, Belzer."

"It's hard to play Ping-Pong in the dark!" Belzer whined.

I led him into the TV room. It was crowded with kids who didn't want to do their homework. They stared like zombies at the big-screen TV.

I saw April-May June, the coolest, hottest girl at Rotten School. And Flora and Fauna, the Peevish twins. And I saw Wes Updood, and Sherman Oaks, and Joe Sweety, and a bunch of other guys. They're all from the dorm we hate—Nyce House.

"Okay, Belzer," I said. "Put the shirts down."

"Bernie, can you help me?" he asked. "They're stacked so high; I don't want to spill them."

"Sorry. I can't. I have muscle cramps," I said.

He stooped low. I could hear his knees crack. He set the shirts and caps on the floor beside the big TV.

"Good work, Belzer," I said. I touched knuckles with him. "Now, step aside and watch a master salesman go to work."

I stepped in front of the TV. "Attention, everyone!" I shouted. "Attention!"

I held up a beautiful Stupid Chicken T-shirt. "I've got the shirts you want!" I shouted. "Don't crowd me. There's plenty to go around!"

"BOOOOOOOOO!"
"HISSSSSSSSS!"

What a strange reaction.

"You're not booing *me*—are you?" I asked. "You're booing something on TV—right?"

I held up a Little Cluck-Cluck cap. "These are *awesome!*" I shouted. "One size fits all. Get your money out!"

"BOOOOOOOOO!"
"HISSSSSSSSS!"

They WERE booing and hissing me!

Is that any way to treat a Hall of Famer? Is that any way to treat the most popular dude on campus, even though I'm too modest to say it myself?

What was this about? Did I do something *wrong?*

Chapter 11

THE CAPED QUACKER

I turned to Wes Updood, the coolest dude in school. "Whussup, Updood?" I asked. "Whussup with the booing and hissing?"

He shrugged. "It's like maple syrup, man," he said. "Drink it from the INSIDE of the bottle, you know? It's sticky like Cincinnati. In your nose, dude. Really."

Wes is so totally cool, no one can understand a word he says!

I took a breath and started over. "Who likes Stupid Chicken?" I asked. "Everybody, right? So who would like to wear the *best* Stupid Chicken T-shirts on earth? They're made of real, genuine, imitation cotton!"

"BOOOOOOOOO!"
"HISSSSSSSSS!"

I could tell it wasn't going well.

And then Joe Sweety, the biggest, meanest kid in school, bounced up from his chair. He stampeded toward me, shaking his huge fist.

"Bernie, I'm gonna punch out your lights!" he snarled.

"Down, boy, down!" I said. "Sit! Sit!"

That always worked with Beast. But Sweety was a little more human.

"Remember the raw hamburger Chef Baloney gave us for lunch that made us all puke our guts out?" he growled. "Well, that's what your *face* is gonna look like!"

I grabbed his big fist as it swung toward me. "I think you have a hangnail," I said. "Let me take a look at that."

My heart was thudding in my chest. I felt weak. Dizzy.

Why did Sweety want to pound me into chopped meat? What did I do wrong?

He pulled his fist back. I could see that it had my name written on it. My whole life flashed before my eyes.

"Someone, please—" I begged. "Tell me! What did I do wrong?"

Joe Sweety lowered his fist. "We HATE Stupid Chicken!" he growled.

"He's totally stupid!" Flora Peevish said with a sneer. "Only babies watch Stupid Chicken."

Sweety pulled the shirt from my hands and ripped it into tiny shreds. "That's what we think of Stupid Chicken," he said.

"YAAAAAAAAAAY!"

Everyone cheered.

I glanced at the TV. "I don't get it," I said. "You're not watching Stupid Chicken? What are you watching?"

Sweety rolled his eyes. "We're watching *Drastic Duck*, of course. What else?"

Excuse me? Drastic Duck?

"The Caped Quacker!" Fauna Peevish exclaimed. "He's Plucked—and he's Pumped—for ACTION!"

"YAAAAAAAAAAY!"

They cheered again, jumping up and down and quacking at the top of their lungs.

Sherman Oaks—that spoiled, rich kid—walked up to me. He flashed me his perfect, million-dollar smile and brushed back his wavy blond hair. His blue eyes sparkled.

"Check these out, Bernie," he said.

He held up a handful of gray feathers. "My parents bought me these feathers. They're worth five thousand dollars."

I squinted at the feathers. They looked like normal feathers to me. "Why are they so valuable?" I asked.

Sherman sneered at me. "It's obvious, isn't it? They came off the *actual duck* used as a model for Drastic Duck. They are the most valuable duck feathers in the world!"

"YAAAAAAAAAAAY!"

The kids in the TV room all cheered again. Then they began to do the Drastic Duck chant:

> "*Drastic is Fantastic!*
> *Drastic is Fantastic!*
> *Drastic is NOT a spastic!*
> *Drastic is Fantastic!*"

They did some more cheering and some more quacking.

When it finally got quiet, I turned back to Sherman. "Let me see those five-thousand-dollar feathers," I said.

He raised them to my face.

The feathers brushed my nose. And—UH-OH!—I ...

SNEEZED!

Whoa. The feathers flew up into the air. The ceiling fan blew them everywhere. I saw some of them sail out the window.

Sherman dove to the floor in a feeble attempt to rescue his precious feathers. He caught two or three of them. He waved his fist at me.

"You did that on purpose!" he shouted. "You did that because you're a Stupid Chicken fan!"

"No. Not true!" I cried. "I couldn't help it! I—I—"

I sneezed again. Sherman's last three feathers went flying out the window.

Kids gasped in horror.

Joe Sweety jumped to his feet. "This means WAR!" he boomed.

Chapter 12

DANGLEPHOBIA

Joe Sweety picked me up by my shirt and pushed me against the wall.

"Want to watch some TV?" I gave him my best smile.

Sweety growled.

All the girls and Nyce House dudes mobbed me, shouting angrily.

I didn't like the way this was going. I'm a popular guy. Popular guys don't like to be pressed against a wall and mobbed.

"You got me wrong!" I shouted. "I *love* Drastic

67

Duck! He's my favorite duck! Really! He's so totally ... *drastic!*" "WAR!"

Sweety bellowed.

"WAR!"
"WAR! WAR! WAR!"

Even April-May was pumping her fists and chanting.

Didn't she know she was my girlfriend? Didn't she know she should be *helping* me?

"Punch him in the encyclopedia!" Wes Updood roared.

That dude is so cool. I wish I could understand him.

"Encyclopedia! Encyclopedia!" Updood started to chant.

But no one joined in on that one.

"Put me down! Put me down!" I shouted at Joe Sweety. "I have Danglephobia! It's very serious. I'm afraid of having my feet dangle in the air!"

Sweety pressed me harder against the wall.

"Sorry, Bernie," he growled. "We have to defend Drastic Duck!" He pushed till it felt like his hand went right through me!

I was rapidly becoming Flat Bernie!

Could things get worse? Yes.

The mob went for my shirts. They knocked over the pile. Then they began grabbing them away.

"Not the shirts!" I cried. "Not the shirts! They cost me big bucks!"

What were these Nyce House creeps doing? I saw them passing around black markers. They spread the shirts on the floor.

They were *drawing* on them!

I couldn't believe it. They were drawing DUCKS all over my Stupid Chicken shirts!

"WAR! WAR! WAR!"

"Encyclopedia! Encyclopedia!"

They quacked and chanted as they destroyed my shirts.

"I'm ruined!" I wailed. "Ruined!"

And then a booming, deep voice silenced everyone:

"LEAVE HIM ALONE!"

Joe Sweety let go of me, and I slid to the floor. Kids dropped the shirts and backed away in silence. They were all trembling.

"THAT'S BETTER!"

the voice boomed.

I lay in a flattened heap on the floor. I looked up and saw the owner of the voice. Jennifer! Jennifer Ecch!

Jennifer is the biggest, meanest, muscliest, hulkiest

girl in school. She's, like, *prehistoric*! I mean like those furry mastodons in our history textbook.

Jennifer once arm wrestled a *car*—and WON!

And did I forget to mention that The Ecch is totally in love with me?

Do you know how embarrassing it is to be in fourth grade and have the hulkiest, muscliest, biggest, meanest girl in school slobbering all over you with wet, smoochy kisses?

Well...tonight I was glad to see her.

She reached down, grabbed the collar of my shirt, and lifted me off the floor with one hand. "Are you okay, Lamby Nose?" she asked.

"Please don't call me Lamby Nose," I begged.

She licked my arm for a minute or two. "You're so sweet, I could eat you up!" she gushed.

"Please don't," I muttered.

She took a big bite out of my arm.

Memo to self: Remember to get more Band-Aids.

Then she jumped up and turned to the crowd of kids. "What's going on? Why are you all picking on Honey Face?" she snarled.

No one spoke. They were all too afraid to answer.

The Ecch gazed at the TV screen. "And why are you watching that stupid duck show?" she demanded.

"It's not stupid," Joe Sweety said softly. "We kinda like Drastic Duck."

"CHANGE THE CHANNEL!"

Jennifer roared. "Are you all crazy? You've got to watch the *best* show!"

"Wh-what's the best show?" Sherman asked.

Jennifer didn't reply. Instead she pulled back her school blazer. And we could all see her T-shirt:

POWER PIGEON!

Chapter 13

HE'S COO-COO-
COOLOSSAL!

"Power Pigeon?" Joe Sweety cried. "You can't be serious, Ecch! You have to be a total *geek* to watch that fat pigeon. He eats *garbage* off the sidewalk!"

"Oh, yeah?" Jennifer sneered. "That's how he gets his COO-COO-COOURAGE!"

"Who wants a superhero that coos?" Sweety said.

"Only coo-coo-cool people!" Jennifer replied. "Let me show you a coo-coo-cool trick I learned on *Power Pigeon*. Did you ever see the episode called 'Knots To You!'?"

She grabbed Sweety around the neck and lifted

him off the floor. Then she began twisting his arms and legs like he was a balloon animal.

In three seconds, she had him tied into a knot. "This is called a Double Shell Bend knot," Jennifer said.

She grabbed Sweety's arms and tucked them around his legs. "And this is a Halyard knot. It's used a lot by fishermen and sailors. Now let me show you my favorite."

She bent and twisted poor Joe's body. "This is a perfect Figure Eight knot," she said. She held him up so everyone could see.

No lie. She bent Sweety into a perfect figure eight. If you put salt on him, he'd look just like a pretzel!

She dropped him to the floor. We all watched him roll away, dazed and defeated. I could hear him out in the hall trying to untangle himself.

"Jennifer—you can't DO that!" Sherman Oaks screamed.

"We have a right to watch *Drastic Duck*!" Flora Peevish shouted. "It's in the Constitution!"

"Oh, yeah?" the Ecch boomed. She made a move

toward Flora. But Angel Goodeboy jumped between them.

Angel looks a lot like an angel. He has shiny blond hair and a round face with pink cheeks and sparkling blue eyes. Sometimes I look for a halo floating over his head.

Angel smiled warmly at Jennifer. "Why can't we all just get along?" he asked. "Let's all be kind to each other."

"I'll show you *my* idea of kind," Jennifer cried.

She lifted Angel off his feet and began shifting his arms and legs. She finished by tucking his head into his body. Then she held him up for everyone to see.

"Look. A box turtle!" Jennifer said.

She set him on the floor, and Angel crawled away slowly.

"Anyone else want to say something bad about the Pigeon of Plutonium?" Jennifer demanded.

"A lightbulb only screws in one way," Wes Updood said.

"Oh, *yeah?*" Jennifer cried.

She dove at Wes. She grabbed his arms and

started to bend him.

But April-May June and her friend Sharonda Davis leaped onto Jennifer. They tugged her off Wes, pushed her to the floor, and tried to sit on her.

And that's when things got out of control.

Some kids started chanting:

"WAR! WAR! WAR!"

Another group began chanting the Drastic Duck Chant:

"Drastic is Fantastic!
Drastic is Fantastic!"

Some of my Rotten House friends came into the TV room and began blucking their heads off.

BLUCK BLUCK BLUCK
GLUCK LUCK BLUCK BLUCK!

That made the Drastic fans quack.

QUACK BLUCK COO

Louder. Louder. Quacking and blucking till the floor vibrated and the walls shook.

Quack Bluck

"Buffalo Wings of Steel!" someone shouted.

Coo BLUCK QUACK

"Webbed Feet of Wonder!"

BLUCK Quack

"Stupid Chicken is a featherbrain!"

QUACK BLUCK Coo

"Stupid Chicken will roast Drastic Duck on a spit!"

Quack Bluck

"Power Pigeon is Coo-Coo-Coolossal!"

COO BLUCK

BLUCK QUACK COO

"QUACK QUACK QUACK ATTACK!"

COO Coo Bluck

"BLUCK BLUCK—You're outta LUCK!"

BLUCK QUACK COO

Then it got REALLY UGLY. With everyone pushing and shoving and twisting and bending and quacking and blucking and fighting and flapping and crying and crowing.

And three guesses who walked in.

You got it. Headmaster Upchuck.

"Bernie," he said. "What's going on here?"

COO Quack

Coo   COO

BLUCK

QUACK

COO   Bluck

Chapter 14

CALM AND QUIET

A hush fell over the room. A few feathers floated down from the ceiling. Nothing else moved.

"What's going on in here?" The Upchuck repeated, glaring at me.

"Nothing, sir," I said. "Just keeping things calm and quiet."

He glared at me some more.

"Keeping it calm and quiet the way you wanted, sir," I said. "We're just hanging out here calmly and quietly. Watching some science shows on TV. You know. Our favorite wildlife documentaries."

He scratched his bald head. "Science documentaries?"

"Yes, it's Newt Week," I said. "We always try to catch the shows about newts. It's like a thrill."

I'm not sure the Headmaster believed me. He gave me the evil eye. "I'm watching you, Bernie. And guess what? I've been practicing cartwheels. Know why?"

"Why, sir?" I asked.

"Because I'm going to do cartwheels across the Great Lawn when I send you home for good!"

"That won't be necessary, sir," I said.

"Remember, Bernie," Upchuck said, "calm and quiet till Parents' Day—or ELSE!" He made a slicing motion across his throat.

"No prob, sir," I said. I flashed him a sharp salute. "We all love calm and quiet around here."

As soon as he was out the door, the war started up again. Clucking and blucking, quacking and hacking, pushing and pecking, flapping and flipping.

Read my lips—it was ugly.

Chapter 15

WHY DOES A CHICKEN HAVE THREE TOES?

The next afternoon, I sat daydreaming in Mrs. Heinie's class. I dreamed about making big money by selling chickens and ducks to Chef Baloney in the dining hall.

Billy the Brain was talking. There's a kid in every class who does all the talking—right? In our class, Billy should be called Billy the Mouth!

"Chickens are very interesting animals," Billy was telling the class. "Did you know that they are actually *hunting* birds? They've just forgotten how to hunt."

Mrs. Heinie yawned. "That's very interesting, Billy," she said.

Billy wasn't finished. "Did you know that chickens are the only animals who prefer to take a bath rather than a shower?"

Mrs. H. frowned at him. "Billy, that's a crock," she said.

"Thank you," Billy replied. "Do you know why chickens only have three toes? Because they're born that way."

"That's enough," Mrs. Heinie snapped. She tossed a piece of chalk across the room and hit Billy right between the eyes.

"I assigned a short story last night," she said. "How many of you read one?" She squinted at us through her thick glasses.

No hands went up.

Mrs. H. picked up another piece of chalk. But she couldn't decide who to throw it at. "Why didn't anyone read a story?" she demanded.

Feenman raised his hand. "Mrs. H.," he said, "there was a *Stupid Chicken* marathon on Chickelodeon last night. Six new episodes."

"Who cares?" Joe Sweety shouted. "The Duckscovery Channel showed four hours of *Drastic Duck*. When it was over, my eyes were burning. I couldn't read."

Crench cupped his hands around his mouth. "Drastic Duck is *fowl*!" he shouted.

"Stupid Chicken eats DIRT!" Flora Peevish yelled.

"Can't we all just get along?" Angel Goodeboy asked.

"BLUCK BLUCK BLUCK BLUCK!"

"QUACK QUACK QUAAAAAACK!"

"Quiet, everyone!" Mrs. Heinie screamed. "Quiet! This is a classroom—not a barnyard!"

"MOOOOOOOO!"

Beast exclaimed. The dude is on his own planet. Mrs. H. keeps him on a leash. But that doesn't keep him from mooing when he feels like it.

"You all have book reports to give," Mrs. Heinie said. "Let's start with Crench."

Crench ducked low in his seat and tried to pretend he wasn't there. Mrs. Heinie had to drag him to the front of the class.

He shoved his hands in his pants pockets. He cleared his throat.

"The book that I read was called *Stupid Chicken vs. Mongoose Fellow*," he said. "It was very exciting. And I'd recommend it to anyone who likes Stupid Chicken."

Mrs. Heinie took off her glasses and rubbed her eyes. "That sounds a lot like a comic book," she said. She waved for Crench to sit down.

"Nosebleed, you're next," she said. "I hope you read something better."

"I can't give my book report," Nosebleed said. "I have a nosebleed."

Mrs. H. called on April-May June next. April-May bounced to the front of the room. She tossed her blond ponytail behind her head.

"My book is called *Drastic Duck Battles Pond Scum*," she said. "It's a very good story about—"

"Stop!" Mrs. Heinie cried. "Did *everyone* in this class read comic books? Didn't *anyone* read a real book?"

No hands. Finally, Billy the Brain spoke up. "I read a *manga* comic in the original Japanese," he said.

"What was it about?" Mrs. H. asked.

Billy shrugged. "Beats me. It was in Japanese!"

Mrs. Heinie let out a shriek and tore at her hair with both hands. "This chicken and duck thing has gone too far!" she screamed.

Not far enough, I thought to myself.

So far, I hadn't made a DIME from it. I had to find a way to raise cash for the parents' snacks and refreshments. If I didn't, The Upchuck would be doing cartwheels across the Great Lawn!

What could I do?

Believe it or not, I got *big help* that afternoon from Angel Goodeboy!

Chapter 16

FLASH!

It was a sunny afternoon as I walked across the Great Lawn. Apples fell from the apple trees, making a pleasant *splat*. Robins pulled fat worms from the grass and slurped them down.

I didn't care. I couldn't enjoy my walk.

Every step I took, Stupid Chicken and Drastic Duck and Power Pigeon stared out at me. It was like they were *following* me!

That's because kids had plastered their posters on every tree and wall. Someone glued a Stupid Chicken poster on the back of the statue of I.B.

Rotten. Someone pasted Drastic Duck posters on all the toilets in the boys' locker room.

Duck and chicken and pigeon posters everywhere I looked. Hundreds of them!

Why did they make me feel so bad? *Because I didn't sell the posters!*

Was I losing my touch?

I was going broke on T-shirts and caps. Why didn't I think of posters?

It was a low moment for Bernie B. And then an apple fell on my head just to make the day perfect.

I was rubbing the juice from my hair when I saw Angel Goodeboy running toward me. He had a big bag in one hand.

"Bernie, oh my gosh and goodness. Can you do me a big favor?" he asked.

"Of course," I said. "Anything for a pal." I eyed the bag. "Do you have candy in there that you'd like to share?"

"Gosh, no. I just refilled all these ink markers. I'm late for my after-school Flower Arranging class. Can you take the markers to Mrs. Twinkler in the art room for me?"

FLASH!

That flash was the great Bernie B. having a brilliant idea.

"Yes. No prob," I said. I took the bag of markers from him. "No prob at all."

"Oh my gosh. Thanks, Bernie," Angel said. He rushed off to his class.

Now I had a grin on my face.

I saw Feenman walking across campus. He stopped to shake his head and frown at a Drastic Duck poster. I hurried over to him.

"They shouldn't be allowed to put that creepy duck up," I said. "Feenman, don't you think he'd look better with a mustache and beard?"

"You got *that* right!" Feenman said. "Wish I had a marker!"

"It's your lucky day," I said. I pulled a marker from the bag. "Only three dollars."

Feenman pulled three dollars from his pocket. I

handed him the marker, and he went to work on the poster. In a few seconds, Drastic Duck had a lovely, black beard and mustache. Across the lawn, I saw April-May in front of a poster of Stupid Chicken. I ran as fast as I could. "They have a lot of *nerve* putting up that poster," I said. "Wouldn't you just love to add a beard and mustache?"

"And maybe make his eyes crossed," April-May

said. "Wish I had a marker."

"Your wish is my command!" I said. I sold her a marker for three dollars.

An hour later, all the markers were sold. My pockets were bulging with dollar bills. And all the posters on campus had beards, mustaches, eyeglasses, and rude words all over them.

A job well done!

But, you know me, dudes. You know that this was just the beginning!

Chapter 17

FLYTRAPS FOR THE UPCHUCK

The next day I told Belzer to get down on the ground and gather up as many pigeon feathers as he could. Then I sold the feathers for a dollar each.

I told Drastic Duck fans they were Official Drastic

Duck Feathers. And you can probably guess what I told Stupid Chicken fans.

It was kinda funny. Kids walking around, proudly showing off their pigeon feathers.

"Belzer, I'm all out of feathers," I said, counting my money. "Find more."

"But, Bernie," he whined, "there *aren't* any more. I searched everywhere."

"Can't you pluck some pigeons?"

"I already did!" he said. "Haven't you seen all the naked birds walking around campus?"

Okay. No prob.

I bought some duck-call whistles. I sold them to Drastic Duck fans for two dollars each.

Then I sold little chicken dolls to the Stupid Chicken fans. Squeeze them and they clucked like

chickens. And I sold birdseed to the Power Pigeon fanatics.

The money rolled in like ... like ... money.

I knew I could cash in on these cluckers and quackers. Why did I ever doubt the great Bernie B.?

One afternoon I was up in my room, lying in bed, counting the huge wad of bills again and again—just for fun.

Three hundred bucks! Whoa. Even I was impressed. That was enough money for snacks and refreshments for the parents. And PLENTY left over for the Bernie Bridges Private Charity Fund.

I jumped to my feet and did a happy dance, waving the money over my head. Could *anything* be better? Could *anything* ruin this moment?

Yes.

Mrs. Heinie stepped into my room. I could tell she was angry. Her glasses were steamed.

"You're looking beautiful today, Mrs. Heinie," I said, flashing her my best smile. "Did you have that wart on your cheek removed? Very smooth!"

She glared at me through her steamy glasses. "Bernie, I've received a very bad report about you," she said. "Angel Goodeboy told me that you stole the black markers from the art room and sold them to kids for three dollars each."

"Huh?"

My mouth dropped open. "Angel Goodeboy? He … he GAVE me the markers!"

Angel was no angel. Angel was a total snitch.

Mrs. Heinie stared at the wad of bills in my hand. "Bernie, stealing is very serious," she said. "Selling school property is also very serious."

It looked bad. But I knew I could think my way out of this.

Think fast, Bernie. Think FAST!

"I'm sorry," Mrs. H. said, shaking her head. "But I have to take you to Headmaster Upchuck and report the whole story."

The whole story?

He'll toss me out of school with a huge grin on his face. He won't even wait till Parents' Day!

"Wait, Mrs. Heinie," I said. "You don't understand. Let me explain."

She crossed her arms and tapped her shoe on the floor. "I'm listening," she said. "This better be good."

"It is," I said. "See this money? Three hundred dollars. It's supposed to be a surprise."

She tapped her shoe faster. "A surprise?"

I nodded. "For Headmaster Upchuck. It's a birthday surprise from all of us guys. He's always wanted his own Venus Flytrap garden in front of his house, right? Well, we raised enough money for fifty Flytraps. He'll be so happy. But it's a secret. We don't want to spoil the surprise."

Was she buying it?

She stared at me, tapping her shoe.

"That's a wonderful surprise, Bernie," she said finally. "Tell you what, I'll take the money and buy the Flytraps for you. You've worked hard. Let *me* do the rest."

"But—but—"

She grabbed the wad of bills from my hand and stuffed it into her pocket. Then she turned and hurried down the stairs.

I stared at the empty doorway, breathing hard. Was she *really* going to use my hard-earned money to buy Flytraps for The Upchuck? Or was she going to buy herself another tattoo?

It didn't matter. I was back where I started. Totally broke. No money for refreshments. No money for my Private Charity Fund.

Was it too late to start over?

Chapter 18

COVER YOUR EARS!

CLUUUUCK, CLUUCK!
HONNNNK, HONNNNK, HONNNK!

The superhero battle raged. No one could stop it now.

In the Dining Hall at lunch, the honking and clucking and cooing made the plates shake on the tables. The sounds echoed off the walls and ceiling of the huge room.

Most kids had to hold their ears while they honked their duck calls or made their chickens cluck or cooed like a loud pigeon.

At a corner table, a group of girls sang the Power Pigeon song at the top of their lungs. I couldn't hear them. The honking and clucking drowned them out.

Everyone was having a great time—until Headmaster Upchuck poked his bald head in. He stormed into the room, red-faced, covering his ears.

I wasn't honking or clucking or chanting or quacking or singing. But, of course, he blamed me!

"Bernie, what's all the *racket?*" he shouted.

I gave him my innocent, wide-eyed look. "Racket, sir? I didn't hear anything."

"You don't hear that *awful noise?*" he boomed.

"I think it's just us digesting our lunch," I said.

The Upchuck shook his fist. "I warned you, Bernie," he growled. "Your job was to keep this school calm and quiet to get everyone ready for Parents' Day. Shall I buy your bus ticket home?"

"Home, sir?" I said. "I don't understand."

"All this clucking and quacking!" the Headmaster said. "I don't call this calm and quiet."

He took my arm. "You failed, Bernie. Come on. Let's get you packed."

Think fast, Bernie. Think fast!

"We're just excited, sir," I said. "We're totally *psyched* about our overnight on an actual farm."

His mouth dropped open. "Overnight? On a farm?" He shook his head. "How come no one ever tells me about these things?"

He walked off muttering to himself.

"Overnight?" Belzer asked. "Bernie, we're going on an overnight to a farm?"

"Of *course* not!" I said. "I made that up. Why would we go on an overnight to a farm?"

FLASH!

There it was. Another brilliant idea.

Chapter 19

Don't Catch the Plague!

That night I called the local farm and ordered one hundred live chickens. I didn't buy them. I just borrowed them.

Why did I borrow a hundred chickens?

What were they for?

Where did I plan to put them?

Questions, questions. Easy-to-answer questions—*if* you have a brilliant brain for scheming and plotting.

And do you know anyone who schemes and plots as well as Bernie B.?

What were my assignments from Headmaster

Upchuck? Keep the school calm and quiet for a week. And raise a ton of money for Parents' Day refreshments.

Well...the best way to keep the school calm and quiet was to put an *end* to the chicken-duck-pigeon war. And maybe someone—namely ME—could put an end to the war *and* make a lot of money at the same time.

That's where the chickens came in.

Are you following me so far?

Well, I called a Rotten House dorm meeting to clue my friends in.

The guys all made their way into the Commons Room, our living room. It took only ten or fifteen minutes for them to fight over who got the couch. Feenman and Crench stood against the wall, making each other flinch.

Mrs. Heinie was out hanging with the motor-cycle gang she rides with every week. So the coast was clear for planning and scheming.

"Dudes, we're gonna end the war," I started.

"Stupid Chicken rules!" Beast declared. He tore off a wooden chair arm and began chewing big chunks out of it. "Stupid Chicken RULES!"

"The Duck is YUCK! The Duck is YUCK!" They all began to chant. "The Duck is YUCK! The Duck is YUCK!"

After an hour or so, they began to get tired of the chant. So I started again.

"Do you know the Nyce House dudes are having a big dance party?" I asked.

They stared at me.

"No. You don't know about it," I said. "Because none of us are invited. It's in the gym on Friday night. They have a dj and everything. Sherman and his pals invited girls from the Girls' Dorm. But we're not allowed in!"

Feenman rolled his eyes. "Like we would go to their stupid party anyway," he muttered. "Hang out with those dudes, you get cooties."

"You get rabies!" Crench said.

"No. You get Booblonic Plague," Billy the Brain said.

"Excuse me?" I said. "What's Booblonic Plague?"

"It's like a disease," Billy said. "It's way dangerous. It rots your booblonic."

"I had it once," Beast said. "Made my hair itch like crazy!"

"Listen, I've got more to tell you guys," I said. "Can you guess the theme of the Nyce House party? It's Drastic Duck."

"The Duck is YUCK! The Duck is YUCK!"

They started chanting again. I had to wait another hour for them to get worn out.

"I think it's time to put an end to Drastic Duck and the whole war," I said finally. "I promised Headmaster Upchuck calm and quiet. And we're gonna get calm and quiet—by starting the biggest, noisiest riot in school history!"

"Sounds like a plan," Billy the Brain said. He flashed me a thumbs-up.

"I've ordered a hundred live chickens," I said. "Listen up, dudes. Here's what we're going to do with them...."

Chapter 20

It Turns into a Surprise Party

Friday night. The Nyce House party in the gym was already underway.

My buddies and I crept up to the back doors of the gym. What did we plan to do?

Crash the party.

Crash the party with our chickens.

Five dollars. That's what it cost my friends to buy their very own chickens.

A great price. What would you pay to ruin a Nyce House party? Any amount, right?

So Bernie B. ended up with a drawer full of cash

for Parents' Day snacks.

And now, my Rotten House friends carried each of their chickens proudly. Hugging them tightly to their chests to keep them quiet.

I pulled open the door to the gym. Loud, thumping music and a roar of voices poured out.

Silently we carried our little surprises into the gym. This was a night the Drastic Duck dudes would never forget.

A hundred squawking, flapping, pecking chickens could ruin *any* party.

The war was about to be won. The Nyce House dudes would learn a new word tonight—*defeat.*

Calm and quiet would be the rule from now on.

And Headmaster Upchuck would thank me for a job well done.

Hugging our chickens, we crept along the back wall of the gym. In the center of the floor, kids danced and joked and hung out.

I gazed around at the decorations. Paintings of Drastic Duck on the walls. Streamers in Drastic Duck colors—gray and dark gray. Clusters of gray and dark gray Drastic Duck balloons.

I waited for the right moment. The moment the music stopped.

"Okay," I said. And I raised my hand high. The signal to let the chickens go.

With a cry of, "Stupid Chicken Rules!" my buddies tossed their chickens high into the air.

AWWWWWWWK!

SQUAWWWWWWWK!

What a racket. The chickens squawked their heads off. And flapped furiously.

Then they hit the floor, running in wild, crazy circles. Flapping their wings. Sliding on the gym floor.

AWWWWWWWK!

SQUAWWWWWWWK!

BLUUUUUUUCK!

The flapping chickens scuttled toward the kids in

the center of the floor. Some kids cried out. They backed away.

That's when I saw the cages against the wall. A long row of gray cages.

What were in those cages?

I saw Sherman and his pals running to the cages. They were pulling open the cage doors.

And I suddenly had a very bad feeling.

How could I know that the Nyce House guys would bring a hundred *ducks* to their party?

Chapter 21

A Thank-You from the Headmaster

I guess the ducks were part of the decorations. Or maybe they were party favors.

Anyway, it wasn't good news.

The ducks came honking out of their cages. They flapped their wings and snapped their bills. And zoomed straight at the squawking chickens.

What can I say?

Feathers flew.

Kids backed against the four walls, staring in horror as a REAL war took place!

HONNNNNK! HONNNNNK!

SQUAWWWWK!
ULLLLP!

Those animals knew how to make a racket.

Flapping and screeching and honking and squawking. Until even I had to hold my hands over my ears.

I saw two ducks fly out the gym window. A chicken scrambled out the open door. Two more chickens followed.

The animals were *escaping* onto the campus.

And of course, that's when Headmaster Upchuck decided to pay a visit to the party.

HONNNNNK!
HONNNNNK!
SQUAWWWWK!

I waited for the look of horror on his face. He *did* turn bright red. But he wasn't scowling or gasping or shrieking.

He was GRINNING.

"Bernie, thank you! Thank you!" he cried. He stepped over a chicken and hurried up to me.

"You don't have to thank me, sir," I said.

"Oh, but I do!" said the Headmaster. His grin grew so wide, it covered his eyes! "Thank you for *finally* giving me a good reason to say bye-bye, Bernie!"

"But—but—"

"You're outta here!" he screamed. "I *knew* you'd fail! I'm booting you out, Bernie! Out of this school! Oh, happy day! You're going home!"

And he did cartwheels from one end of the gym to the other.

Chapter 22

THE SCHOOL IS RUINED!

"But, sir—" I chased after him.

Kids were screaming and running after the chickens and ducks. I saw Joe Sweety wrestling with two ducks. They had him pinned to the floor. But he was putting up a good fight.

Across the floor, Beast grinned at me. He had chicken feathers stuck to his teeth.

Uh-oh.

Even Beast wouldn't eat a *live* chicken—would he?

Ducks flew out the windows. Kids struggled to catch chickens and shove them into the duck cages.

I ran across the gym to Headmaster Upchuck. I knew I could talk my way out of this one, if he gave me a chance.

I decided to play innocent. "Sir, I don't understand what I did wrong."

He tossed back his bald head and laughed. "Wrong? Wrong? Do you remember the words CALM and QUIET? I gave you an assignment, Bernie. I didn't ask you to turn my school into a *petting zoo!*"

"I know, sir, but—"

"Let me repeat. Your job was to keep this campus calm and quiet," Upchuck continued. "And to raise money for the Parents' Day refreshments tomorrow."

My mouth dropped open. "Excuse me? *Tomorrow?*"

Upchuck scowled. "When the parents get here tomorrow, they'll think they're in a BARNYARD!"

"B-but, sir—" I sputtered.

"The school is RUINED!" Upchuck shrieked. "RUINED! And it's all your fault, Bernie!"

Most kids would feel bad after hearing an angry speech like that. Most kids would lower their heads in shame. Or maybe start to cry. Or beg the Headmaster for mercy.

Not Bernie B. Not a Hall of Famer.

I flashed Upchuck my best grin.

"Actually, sir," I said, "I think you should congratulate me."

"Huh?" A chicken landed on his head. He batted it away.

"You should congratulate me for saving the school," I told him. "Actually, you might call me a HERO!"

Another chicken landed on him. I think they wanted to hatch his bald head!

He batted the chicken away. "You? A hero?" he cried. "Look at this place! Look what you've done in time for Parents' Day! You're a disgrace! A DISGRACE! How can YOU be a hero?"

My grin grew wider. "Sir," I said, "I forgot to mail out the invitations!"

ABOUT THE AUTHOR

R.L. Stine graduated from Rotten School with a solid D+ average, which put him at the top of his class. He says that his favorite activities at school were Scratching Body Parts and Making Armpit Noises.

In sixth grade, R.L. won the school Athletic Award for his performance in the Wedgie Championships. Unfortunately, after the tournament, his underpants had to be surgically removed.

After graduation, R.L. became well known for writing scary book series such as The Nightmare Room, Fear Street, Goosebumps, and Mostly Ghostly, and a short story collection called Beware!

Today, R.L. lives in New York City, where he is busy writing stories about his school days.

For more information about R.L. Stine,
go to www.rottenschool.com
and www.rlstine.com